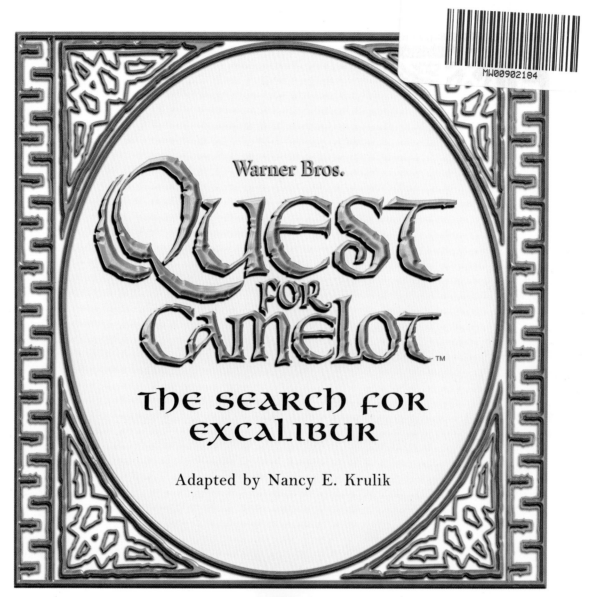

Warner Bros.

QUEST FOR CAMELOT ™

THE SEARCH FOR EXCALIBUR

Adapted by Nancy E. Krulik

WORLDWIDE PUBLISHING ™

SCHOLASTIC INC.

New York   Toronto   London   Auckland   Sydney

ISBN 0-590-12064-6

12 11 10 9 8 7 6 5 4 3 2 1   8 9/9 0 1 2 3/0

Designed by Joan Ferrigno

Printed in the U.S.A.

First Scholastic printing, May 1998

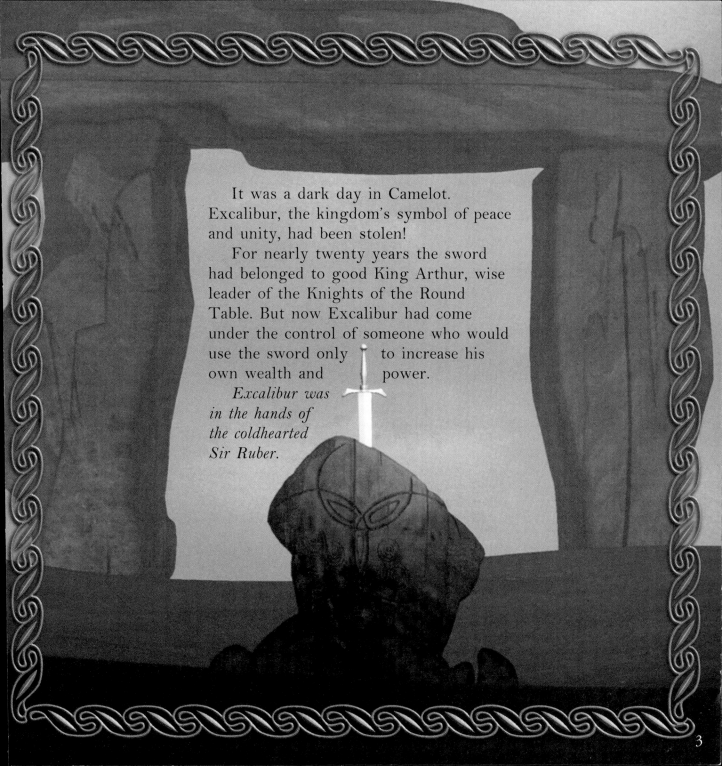

It was a dark day in Camelot. Excalibur, the kingdom's symbol of peace and unity, had been stolen!

For nearly twenty years the sword had belonged to good King Arthur, wise leader of the Knights of the Round Table. But now Excalibur had come under the control of someone who would use the sword only to increase his own wealth and power.

Excalibur was in the hands of the coldhearted Sir Ruber.

Sir Ruber was a hated man. And rightly so. He'd hurt or killed many people in his long quest for power, and for Excalibur. One of the people he'd killed was Sir Lionel, a faithful Knight of the Round Table.

Sir Lionel's teenage daughter, Kayley, vowed to defeat Ruber and protect the ideals her father had died for. Kayley knew her father would have risked everything to retrieve Excalibur and return it to King Arthur.

And that was just what Kayley intended to do.

But Kayley had no idea where the sword was.

As it turned out, neither did Ruber. Kayley overheard Ruber speaking with his Griffin, a terrifying beast with the head and wings of an eagle and the body of a lion. The sound of Ruber's voice sent chills through Kayley's body.

"Excuse me—you lost Excalibur?" Kayley heard Ruber shout out.

"I was attacked by a falcon," the Griffin explained, nervously choking on his words. "A falcon with silver wings. In a place of untold danger . . . "

"The Forbidden Forest!" Ruber completed the Griffin's sentence. "How totally stupid you are! Excalibur is the one thing that can keep me from my conquest of Camelot!"

Kayley shuddered. *The Forbidden Forest!* Everyone knew that no one emerged from there alive.

Most people would have been frightened off the search right then and there. Kayley would have avoided it too—only she couldn't. She tried to run to Camelot, and warn King Arthur of Ruber's evil scheme. But Ruber's minions blocked her path. Kayley was forced into the Forbidden Forest.

As Kayley raced through the woods, she awakened the bizarre creatures that lived there. Snakelike plants with glaring eyes, living, breathing "mud," and pond monsters with rows of snapping, glaring teeth came to life all around Kayley. And behind her were the scary minions sent by Ruber to capture her.

Turning back to look at the beasts, Kayley tripped, fell down a hill, and tumbled into a nearby lake. There she found herself held prisoner by a fishing net!

"Hey! That's my net!" an angry young fisherman screamed at her.

Before Kayley could reply, a bird with a bladed beak—one of Ruber's minions—soared straight for the young man's head.

Instantly, the young man leaped out of the way. The blade-beaked creature landed blade-first in a tree trunk. A falcon flew to the young man's side and began chirping wildly, signaling more danger to come!

Kayley watched with amazement as Spike Slinger and Bowhands— two more of the creatures— bombarded the young man. Spike Slinger swung his macelike arms. Bowhands used his bowlike hands to shoot arrows with incredible aim. Time after time, the young man leaped out of their way just as they were about to deliver a fatal blow.

Suddenly, the young man went on the offensive! First, he knocked Spike Slinger into a pond monster. The ravenous monster devoured Spike Slinger whole. Then the young man threw Bowhands into a mound of land. The mound came to life and swallowed Bowhands with its enormous mouth.

Kayley freed herself from the young man's net and stood to shake his hand. "That was incredible!" she complimented him.

The young man ignored her praise. He fished his torn net from the stream and frowned. "It took me six weeks to make this!" he complained as he walked away.

"No, wait!" Kayley called after him. "What's your name?"

"It's Garrett," he replied without stopping.

Kayley raced down the path and blocked his way. "I'm Kayley," she introduced herself. Garrett stopped short, but he appeared to stare right past her.

Something in Garrett's eyes made Kayley pause. "Oh, I didn't realize you were . . . "

"Tall? Rugged? Handsome?" Garrett suggested.

"Blind," Kayley said quietly.

Garrett shrugged. "You know, I always forget that one," he murmured as he walked away once more with his chirping falcon by his side.

Kayley took a good look at the falcon. The bird was huge and majestic with smooth silver wings.

Silver wings! Kayley nearly shrieked with delight. "Your falcon has silver wings. It means he knows where Excalibur is!" she told Garrett.

"Sure he does, in Camelot. You know, big castle, lots of flags," Garrett said sarcastically.

"No it's not," Kayley differed. "It's somewhere in the forest. Ruber stole it."

Garrett agreed that Excalibur needed to be returned to King Arthur. He and his falcon, whose name was Ayden, joined Kayley's search. Before long they found themselves in one of the most dangerous areas of the Forbidden Forest . . . dragon country!

Kayley and Garrett heard a mighty *ROAR* coming from above. A dragon swooped down toward them with its flaming jaws cracked wide open! Ayden chirped a warning to his master.

Instinctively, Garrett dove into an abandoned dragon's nest, pulling Kayley with him. Together they crouched inside one of several empty eggshells. After a few moments, the dragon disappeared. Kayley breathed a sigh of relief. They were safe.

Or were they? As Kayley turned her head, she noticed two large shadows on the wall. "DRAGONS!" she cried out.

"Where?!" one of the creatures asked nervously. "I don't see any dragons!"

Kayley was confused. "But you're dragons," she replied, searching in the dark for the monsters.

"Let me handle this," one dragon ordered the other. Suddenly his ferocious-looking shadow rose on the wall.

"Good show, Corny," the other dragon said. "Let me have a go." The other dragon made a shadow on the wall. But *his* shadow looked like a little bunny.

"Oh, great. The *bunny* of death." The first dragon laughed sarcastically at the shadow puppet. "They're probably cringing in fear."

Garrett and Kayley heard shouts and thumps as the dragons tried to beat each other up.

Garret approached the dragons and knocked away the shell they were hiding behind. Kayley was astonished to see that they were really *one* dragon with two heads.

"Please don't hurt us," one begged.

"I thought you were ferocious dragons," Garrett teased.

"Not exactly," said the other. "The real ferocious ones are those fire-breathing bullies out there."

The dragons rose to their feet and dusted themselves off.

"I'm Devon . . . and this growth on my neck is Cornwall," one dragon head remarked. Soon the two of them were bickering again.

Garrett looked disgusted. "C'mon, Kayley," he called. He strode away purposefully, with Kayley right behind him.

Devon and Cornwall were puzzled. "Hey, where are you going?" Cornwall yelled.

"To save Camelot," Kayley replied.

Camelot? The dragons were instantly intrigued. Both Devon and Cornwall wanted very much to go to Camelot.

Suddenly, vicious fire-breathing dragons appeared in the sky. Devon and Cornwall screamed and prepared to hide. Then they remembered Kayley and Garrett.

"If we help them, they might take us to Camelot," Cornwall said.

"Well, let's save the humans then," Devon agreed.

They led the group to the only exit from dragon country—a narrow stone path that stretched across a scalding acid lake.

Garrett placed his staff at the edge of the water. The staff sizzled. "Is this lake safe?" he asked Cornwall.

"So long as you don't step in it," Cornwall replied.

Garrett had no choice. He could hear the fiery dragons flying closer. Using his staff to guide him, the blind man followed the others across the lake.

Cornwall pointed at something in alarm. "Yikes, it's another dragon!"

But it wasn't a dragon. It was the Griffin and Ruber with his minions! Quickly, Devon and Cornwall directed everyone toward a cave where they would be safe.

"Well the good news is, we're out of dragon country," Garrett told Devon and Cornwall. "The bad news is, this is where we say good-bye."

Devon looked anxious. "You can't leave us here!" he begged.

"If we try to go back, we'll be banished. Ostracized. Exiled," Devon explained.

"Not to mention kicked out," Cornwall added. "We just broke the dragon's cardinal rule: Never help a human."

Kayley took pity on the poor dragons. "Garrett, let's take them with us. *Please*," she pleaded.

Garrett sighed. "Oh, I suppose so," he agreed.

The group journeyed on. Suddenly, Ayden began chirping frantically. He flew over to a mountain ledge and began circling the area. Kayley raced over to the ledge. There she found a cloth strap hanging from a vine.

"Look! This must be from Excalibur!" she exclaimed. "But where's the sword?"

"Someone must have taken it." Garrett tapped at the ground with his staff. "Someone . . . or *something*," he added nervously.

Garrett's tapping revealed that he and Kayley were standing in a giant footprint.
What kind of monster could have made this track? he wondered.

"Now I'll never find Excalibur in time!" Kayley moaned.

"If we follow these tracks we will," Garrett assured her.

Kayley nodded. No matter what kind of monster it was, she had to get Excalibur back.
Soon, the group was bravely walking in the direction of the giant tracks.

Suddenly, Kayley stopped short. "Uh-oh. We've lost the tracks," she explained to Garrett.

Her voice was drowned out by a loud rumbling. Kayley turned nervously to the dragons. "Tell me that was your stomach," she said.

Devon and Cornwall stared accusingly at one another.

"No. Just the Ogre," Garrett explained.

Cornwall's eyes bugged. "An Ogre!" he exclaimed. "Well, see ya! Good luck. Have a nice life . . . whatever's left of it."

Kayley looked confused. "What's so scary about Ogres?" she asked.

"Their appetites," Devon told her.

Before Kayley could ask any more questions, a giant foot loomed overhead. "Get out of the way!" Garrett ordered as the Ogre took another step.

The group scattered as the Ogre's foot touched down. They hid and waited for the giant monster to pass by them. As the Ogre walked along, a leather scabbard fell to the ground.

Kayley looked down at the scabbard. It was just like the one her father had described Excalibur being kept in. "He *does* have Excalibur," she declared.

Now they knew where the sword was. But how were they going to get it back?

Garrett had a plan. "Ogres sleep in the day," he told the group. "We'll wait for him to fall asleep and then we'll grab the sword."

Devon and Cornwall were alarmed. "Define *we*," they said dubiously.

Garrett led the way through a dark tunnel that led to the Ogre's lair. The tunnel fed into an enormous cavern with walls that were peppered with holes. Kayley peered through one of the holes. She could see that the Ogre was falling asleep with Excalibur in his grip. She whispered, "There's a ledge that hangs just above the sword, but it must be a twenty-foot drop."

Quickly, Kayley scrambled up onto the ledge. Garrett and the dragons followed close behind. Garrett, Cornwall, and Devon formed a chain. They took hold of Kayley's legs and gently lowered her toward the Ogre's hand.

Kayley reached out and touched Excalibur. She started to ease the sword from the Ogre's mouth. And then, suddenly . . .

AAACHOOO! Someone let out a sneeze. The Ogre's eyes blinked open.

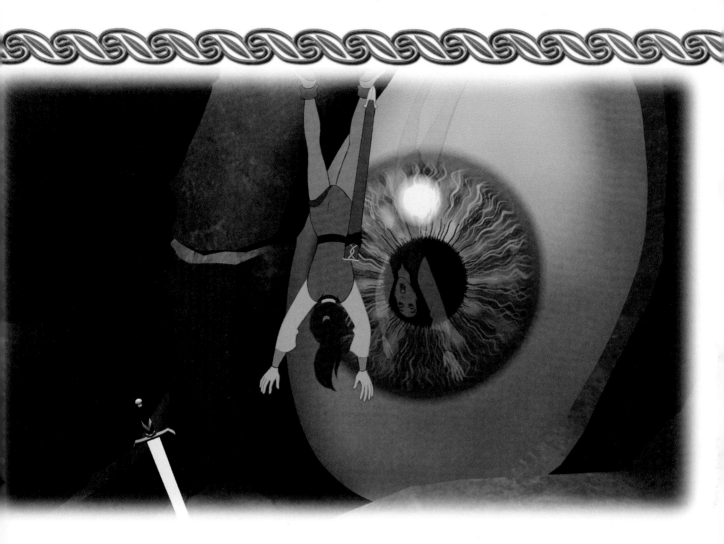

Kayley thought fast. "Nap time's over," she called to Garrett. "Quick! Swing me back and forth!"

Garrett did as he was told. He moved Kayley like a pendulum. "You are getting very sleepy," Kayley whispered hypnotically to the Ogre.

Kayley's plan worked. The Ogre shut his eyes and let out a mighty snore. Quickly, Kayley yanked the sword from his fist and gave the signal. Garrett and the dragons pulled her to the ledge.

But Kayley was still not safe, for the sneeze had come from Ruber's Griffin. The evil knight and his beast had followed them to the Ogre's lair. At that very moment, they were coming toward her. Kayley began to run. Her friends followed close behind.

But Ruber was gaining on them.

Suddenly the Ogre yawned. The forceful burst of air sent Ruber and his Griffin flying. They landed with a thud on the ground. The Ogre stretched and rolled over—pinning Ruber and the Griffin beneath his huge rear end.

Kayley and her friends ran until they reached the end of a mountain cliff. Now there was no way out—unless Cornwall and Devon could fly them to safety. Kayley and Garrett leaped on the dragon's back. They flapped their wings and . . .

Nothing happened. "Houston, we have a problem," Cornwall said.

A *big* problem. Ruber and the Griffin had broken free.

Immediately, the Griffin spotted Ayden and darted after the big bird. At the last moment, the falcon flew out of his way. The Griffin smacked into the side of a mountain. An avalanche of boulders landed on Ruber's head!

"Assume the crash position," Cornwall warned Kayley and Garrett as the dragons slid down the mountain of fallen rocks and safely out of the Forbidden Forest.

"On to Camelot!" Garrett cheered. "Excalibur shall be returned to the hands of Arthur."

And so it was.